HOW TO DRAW
FUNNY
MONSTERS

BARBARA SOLOFF LEVY

DOVER PUBLICATIONS, INC.
Mineola, New York

Note

This book is full of monsters, but the nice part is that they're funny, not scary! Whether it's five legs, three heads, or one gigantic eye, each monster will give you something to laugh about.

To draw each picture, you will follow four steps. The first step will show you how to draw the basic shapes to make the monster. The next three steps will show you the details to add to your picture.

You may want to trace the steps first, just to get a feel for drawing. Then you can make your drawing, using a pencil in case you need to erase some of the lines later on. Be sure to use the helpful Practice Pages, opposite the drawing pages. For the last step of some of the drawings, carefully shade in part of the picture. Also, erase any dotted lines that you made. You can go over the solid lines with a felt-tip marker or a colored pencil. Have even more fun by coloring your drawings with crayons, colored pencils, or markers.

After drawing the funny monsters in this book, you may decide to create some of your own. Have fun!

Bibliographical Note

How to Draw Funny Monsters is a revised republication of the edition first published by Dover Publications, Inc., in 2004. A practice page has been added for each drawing.

International Standard Book Number
ISBN-13: 978-0-486-47493-9
ISBN-10: 0-486-47493-3

Manufactured in the United States by Courier Corporation
47493304   2015
www.doverpublications.com

HOW TO DRAW
FUNNY MONSTERS

2   Funny Monsters

Practice Page

Practice Page

Practice Page

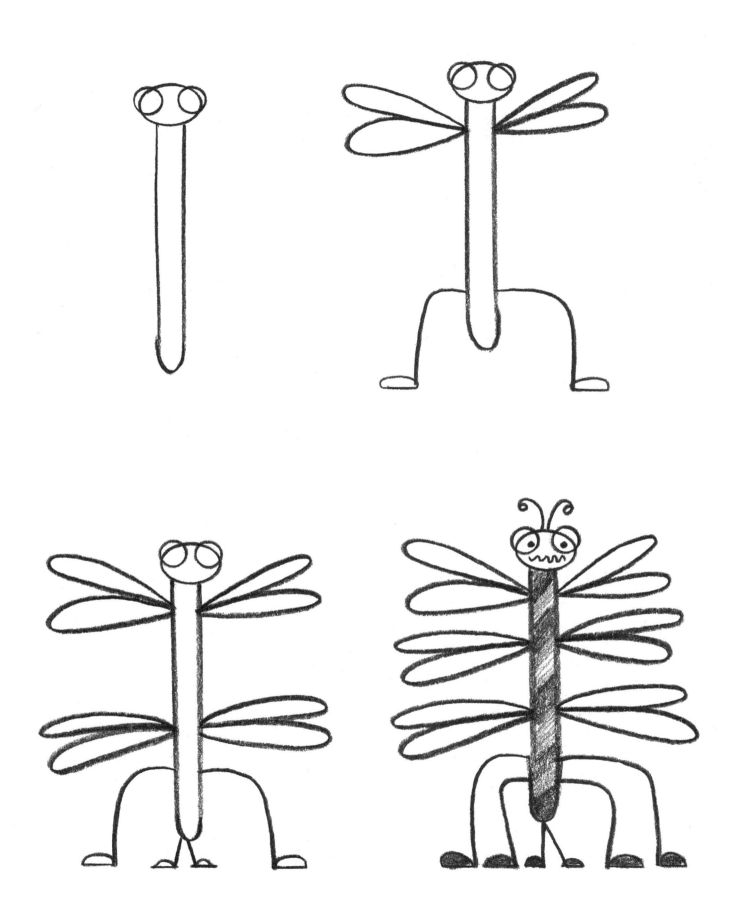

Practice Page

Practice Page

Practice Page

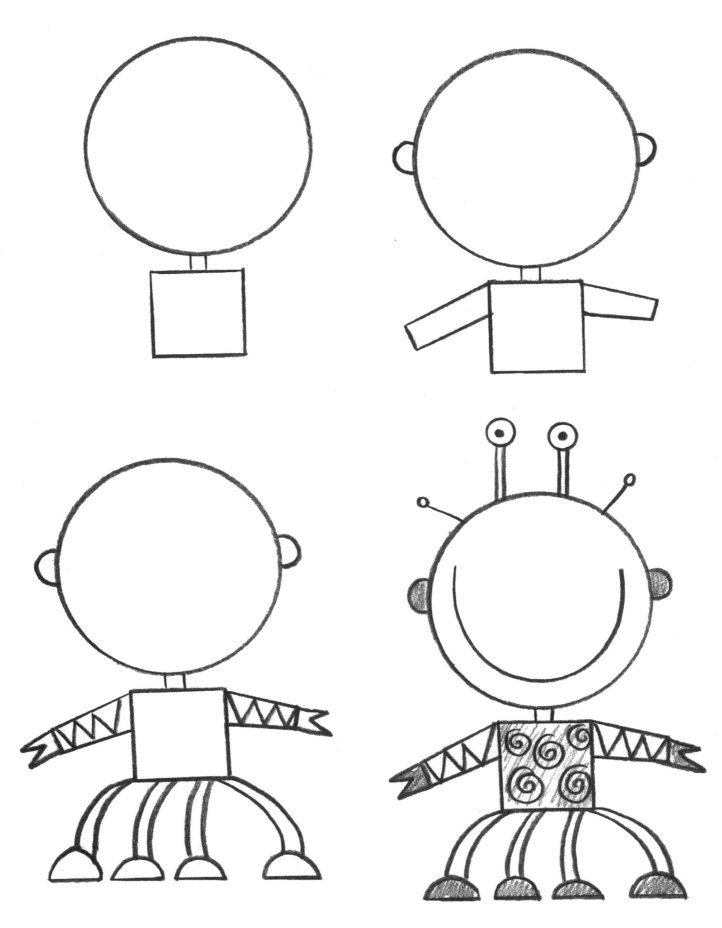

Practice Page

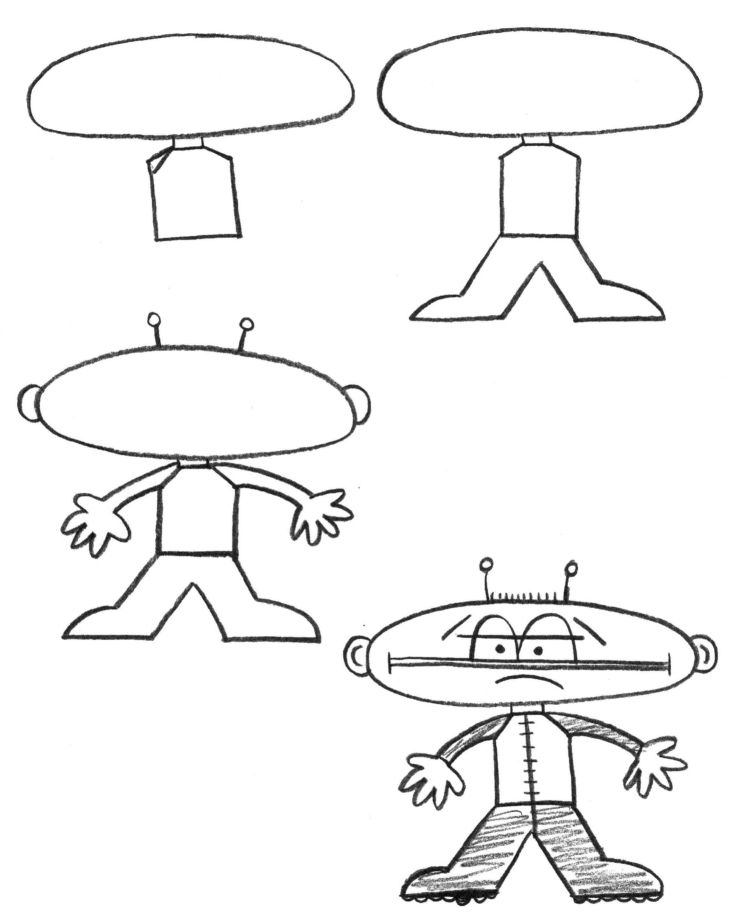

Practice Page

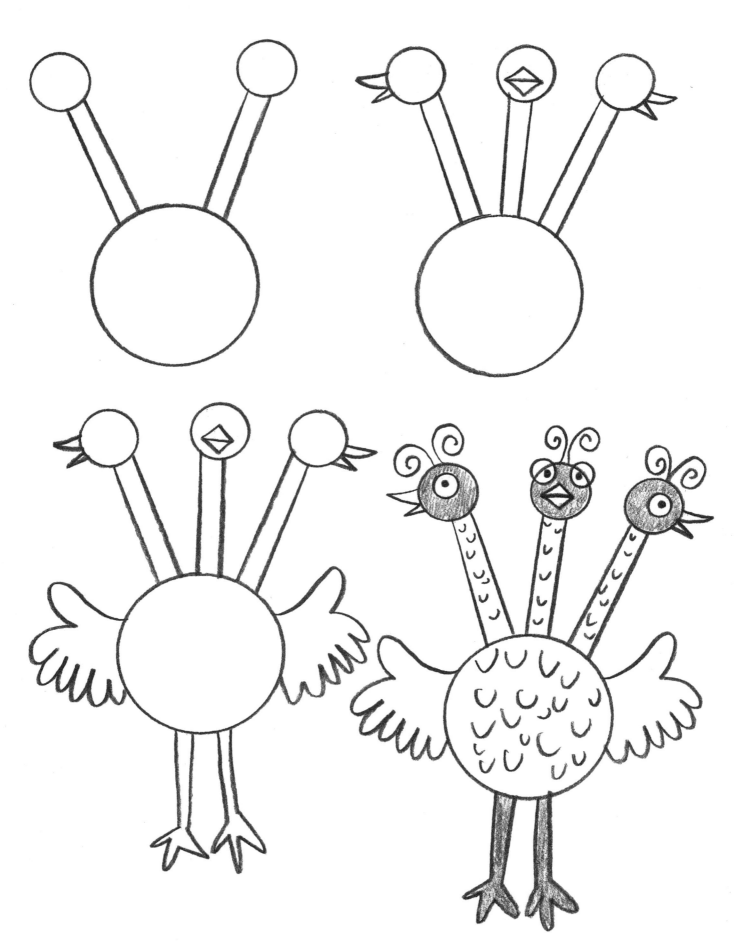

Practice Page

Practice Page

Practice Page

Practice Page

Practice Page

Practice Page

Practice Page

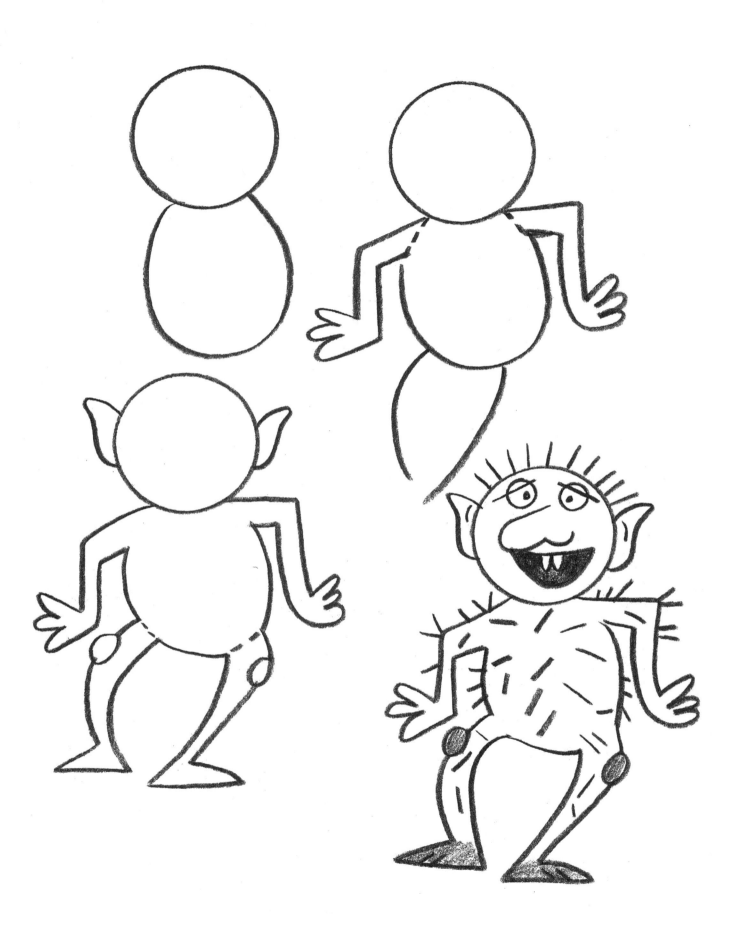

Practice Page

Practice Page

Practice Page

Practice Page

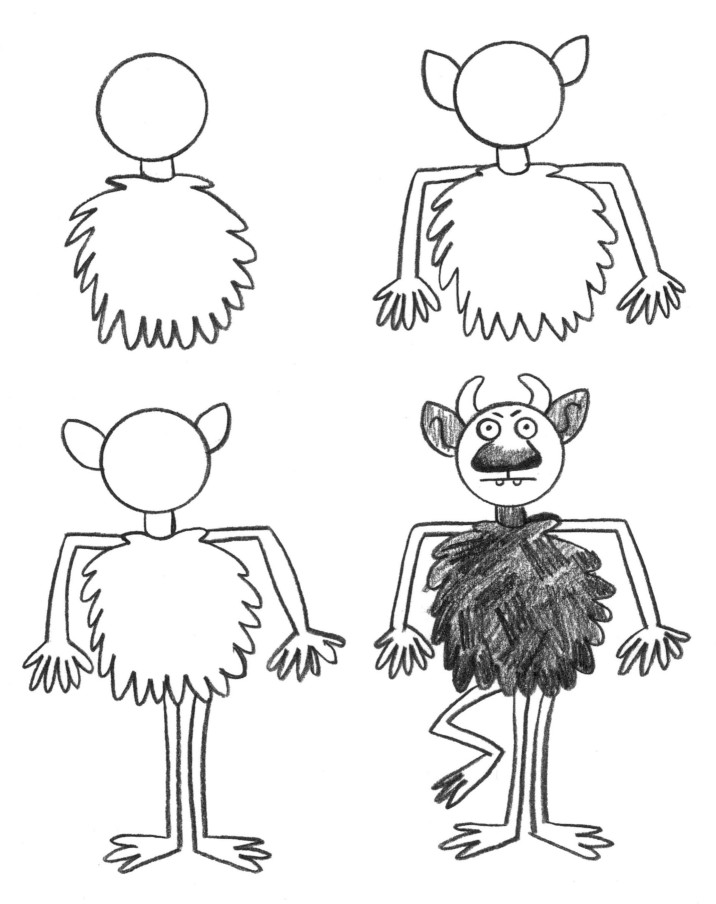

Practice Page

Practice Page

Practice Page

Practice Page

Practice Page

Practice Page

Practice Page

Practice Page